I0714424

Oh, Radio

by

P. Calavara

Here's a fun fact in haiku form:
Pee upon a frog
and if you are now pregnant
the frog will lay eggs.

To Nikola Tesla
or anyone who can tell a
resistor from a transistor

John had a radio on his head.

It had started young as headphones.
Crazy 8-year-old fetish. But as he
got older even walkie talkies and
cell phones equipped with those
wacky little earpieces were too passé.

So John got some welding equipment and a soldering iron, then went to town.

John's head only got three stations. Three and a half if you counted the nearby college NPR feed. But since that was mostly static except when it rained, John didn't usually bother to count it, at least not on a first date. The other three stations were 91.3, 97.7 and for some strange reason, 108.9, which mostly played light jazz.

The music soothed John but the news
was a never-ending parade of negativity.
It seemed the end of the world was
coming. The end of the world made
John anxious. He would lay in bed
listening to updates and the quick-
flash news reports, which interrupted
his relaxing tunes with tragedy
tragedy tragedy.

In order to power the radio in his head, John had to run some 3 miles every day. This he did every morning at the park near his home. Running to morning rock, stepping in beat to the tune as he checked out the people playing tennis in hot pants.

John's intent had never been to use the radio to get sex, but that's sort of how it worked out. Girls in night-clubs, boys at grocery stores, girls on the subway (where the reception sucked), and boys who came by his house selling subscriptions. They all wanted a piece of his exotic allure. Maybe they got a little shock. Maybe they could hear the radio too.

The news got progressively worse and they played music less and less often. And when they did play music, it was always dedicated to someone who had died.

Sex became a hassle for John. No one cared about him, he felt. They just wanted the radio on his head. They just wanted to steal his ideas. He became paranoid: isolating himself behind locked doors in private, and pretending to read in public. He no longer went to nightclubs, which was just as well, as they were all closed because of the tragedy.

John was taking a shower one morning after his run when he slipped on a washcloth, banging his radio on the shower fixture. He lay in a pool of soapy blood and swore that he could hear alien transmissions on a new station he had discovered. He warned the police, but they lacked the resources to do anything. They laughed at him.

John's worst fears were confirmed
one day while shopping for hats. He
had just found a nice knit cap when
he saw a crowd gathered around
Tami, an ex-lover of his.

She turned to him to wave and he
saw the television on her head.
Right then he knew for sure that she
had never really loved him.

The tragedies got worse. Entire countries disappeared into the ocean or, if landlocked, were swallowed by volcanic civil war.

John quit sleeping.

The alien chatter picked up, more and more of it coming through John's head. It only came to him while in the shower or when he drank mint tea. The alien cackling worried him a great deal, but John could not bring himself to stop listening, taking shower after shower after shower.

John began stalking Tami. Observing her movements and eager to get back at her. She had used him to gain his thoughts, to steal his ideas. Sure, she only got Telemundo and Public Access Riverdale, but she was all the rage. John watched all his old lovers take her home and John hated her for it.

He sought therapy for his negative emotions. "Reactionary" and "perfectly reasonable" given "current events" he was told. His counselor recommended he take a break. Head to the country. Camping, maybe. Out of reception. Far from the city.

John went reluctantly from his precious signals but, soon, found himself enjoying the solitude. Enjoying the squirrels and deer and fish that laughed at his quaint, urban attempts to build fire out of sticks and stones. He didn't hear the radio. He didn't see Tami. He didn't hear the tragedies. He was happy.

When his supply of matches ran low
and his two-week vacation dwindled,
John decided it was time to head back
home. He drove slowly, savoring the
ride, not noticing the smoking crater
where the city had been until he had
practically driven into it. The radio
in his head was static. He stared at
the vast expanse of emptiness that
had been his home.

John tried all his stations and finally found one long, sad dirge. A cry of grief for civilization or a country song, sung by the aliens in his head. John lay down.

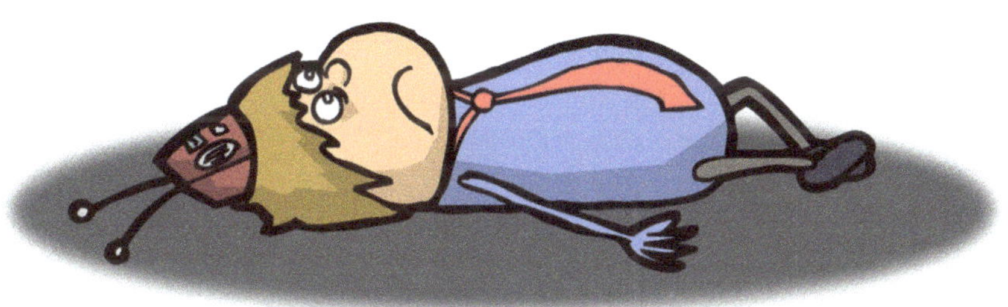

And

With one last surge of power

Listened to the stars.

P. Calavara is an artist
and author in Olympia, WA.

Calavara.com   NeverKnows.com